# Ollie Jolly, Rodeo Clown

Jo Harper ★ ILLUSTRATED BY Amy Meissner

WESTWINDS PRESS®

LIBRARY OF CONGRESS CATALOGING-IN-PUBLICATION DATA
Harper, Jo.
  Ollie Jolly, rodeo clown / written by Jo Harper; illustrated by Amy Meissner.
    p.cm.
  Summary: Ollie Jolly's school assignment is to describe what he wants to be when he grows up, but he has no idea what to write about until he helps a traveling rodeo clown.
    ISBN 1-55868-552-9—ISBN 1-55868-553-7 (pbk.)
      [1. Clowns—Fiction. 2. Cowboys—Fiction. 3. Occupations—Fiction.
    4. Rodeos—Fiction. 5. West (U.S.)—Fiction.] I. Meissner, Amy, ill. II. Title.
PZ7.H23135 O1 2002
[E]—dc21                                    2002023468

WestWinds Press®
An imprint of Graphic Arts Center Publishing Company
P.O. Box 10306, Portland, Oregon 97296-0306
503-226-2402
www.gacpc.com

President/Publisher: Charles M. Hopkins
Associate Publisher: Douglas A. Pfeiffer
Editorial Staff: Timothy W. Frew, Tricia Brown, Ellen Harkins Wheat, Jean Andrews,
        Kathy Matthews, Jean Bond-Slaughter
Production Staff: Richard L. Owsiany, Susan Dupere
Editor: Michelle McCann
Designer: Andrea L. Boven, Boven Design Studio Inc.

Printed in Singapore

For Bobbie, Molly, and Therese—JH

In memory of Charles Meissner, his six-string Mason,
and his fine cowboy songs.—ACM

Ollie Jolly was a comical kid.
Dimple Davis tittered when she saw him
coming down the street. Gracie Garcia
got the giggles as he passed by. Buck Bell
chortled whenever Ollie said, "Howdy!"
Ollie Jolly gave folks the grins.
It wasn't that Ollie was silly.
It wasn't that Ollie was dumb. It
wasn't even that Ollie looked odd. Fact
is, he was cute as a frolicsome Appaloosa
colt—that is, if you like freckles and
chuckles and kinky red hair.
Whenever folks looked in his jolly
face, they couldn't help it.
They laughed. Just seeing Ollie Jolly
made them merry.

Every living soul in the town of Tahoka warmed up to Ollie—all except Shoat Shotley and Miss Tut Tuttle.

Shoat Shotley was a rotten egg. He lived for meanness. He opened a bag of frogs into the choir while they were singing. He sneaked into the cafeteria and poured hot glue in the soup. He broke baby Bessie Mae Miller's new birthday toys just for the heck of it.

And when he laughed, he snorted like a pig.

Shoat hated Ollie just because everyone else loved him.

Miss Tut Tuttle was the meanest teacher in town. She never laughed, not even a snort. She was dour. She was sour. She was a lemon through and through. Just thinking about her made Ollie's mouth pucker up.

One day she said that everyone in class must write a paper on "What Occupation I Will Choose and Why."

Ollie couldn't think of a single job that would suit him, so he started up to Miss Tut Tuttle's desk to ask for help.

On his way he winked at Dimple Davis. He wiggled his ears at Gracie Garcia. He made a face at Buck Bell. And he tripped over Shoat Shotley's foot!

$\mathcal{O}$llie had to give a little skip to keep from falling,

  . . . and somehow, that little skip turned into a dance,

  . . . and the dance led to a few tricks.

  Soon the other kids were roaring with friendly laughter. But not Shoat Shotley. He snorted like a mean pig.

  Miss Tut Tuttle looked more sour than ever. She gave Ollie a cold stare that shot icicles into his jolly heart.

  That stare took the starch right out of Ollie. He sagged like a frost-bitten sunflower and drooped back to his seat.

"Ollie, you don't look the least bit jolly," Dimple said after class. "You look plumb down in the git-alongs."

"I reckon you can see my feathers dragging," Ollie answered. "I need some help, but I can't face Miss Tut Tuttle. She gives me cold feet. I'm so chicken I'm about to cheep."

Dimple giggled. "Shoot, Ollie, you can't let her buffalo you. Let's go to the Dixie Cup Ice Cream Parlor. That'll get your freckles dancing again."

When they got there, the town was full of
horse trailers and cattle trucks. It was rodeo time.
 Cowboys mosied down the street.
 Cowgirls swapped stories in the park.
 Rodeo fans chewed the fat in the
ice cream parlor.

**G**racie Garcia was talking to a lanky, long-legged man. "Meet my new friend, Limber Lem," she said.

Lem started to bow, but he fell right over. Instead of getting up, he stood on his hands and waved his feet in the air.

Everybody was laughing.

"Limber Lem is the bravest man in the rodeo," Gracie said. "He's the clown. He saves the cowboys when they get in trouble, and he makes people laugh while he's doing it."

Behind the crowd, Ollie saw a shadow dart between the trailers. "Uh-oh . . . Shoat Shotley's here," he told Dimple.

"That spells trouble!" Buck Bell said.

With a **BANG**, Shoat Shotley yanked open a trailer and out charged a Brahma bull. He was big enough to shade an elephant and fast as a Texas tornado.

The cowboys let out a holler and skedaddled.

"That's Bad Medicine," Lem told Ollie. "He's the meanest bull in the rodeo!"

Bad Medicine ran straight toward the Dixie Cup.

Dimple Davis gasped. Gracie Garcia screamed. Buck Bell yelled, "Look out!"

Shoat Shotley snickered and snorted.

aving his arms, Limber Lem dashed toward Bad Medicine. The bull swerved and turned on Lem. The rodeo clown leaped aside just as the bull sailed past him, but his boot landed smack dab on a blob of ice cream. Lem staggered, and slipped, and down he went.

Lem was out cold, and Bad Medicine charged again! This was no joke.

"Lem's in a heap of trouble!"
Ollie yelled and jumped into action.
He danced and waved his arms just like
Limber Lem.

Quick as a winter wind, Bad Medicine
swerved toward Ollie.

"*Run Ollie!*" Dimple yelled.

But Ollie didn't run.
Instead he danced and pranced around Bad Medicine.
He turned cartwheels like a rolling tumbleweed.
He hopped and jumped like his middle name was
Jackrabbit.

Soon that bull was muddled, befuddled, and downright confused.

Ollie Jolly leaped into the air,

. . . grabbed the bull by the horns,

. . . flipped over his head,

. . . bounced off his back,

. . . and landed right on Shoat Shotley!
Ollie knocked the wind clean out of his sails. Shoat didn't let
out even the teeniest snort.

The wranglers roped Bad Medicine, and Shoat Shotley limped away, snuffling.

Limber Lem dusted himself off. "Much obliged, Ollie Jolly," he said. "You are brave as a barrel full of bears, and good for grins to boot!"

When the rodeo crew left, Dimple and Ollie ate ice cream and watched the sun go down.

"Ollie Jolly, you aren't one bit chicken," Dimple said. "You faced Bad Medicine, and you can face Miss Tut Tuttle."

But Ollie shook his head.

"Miss Tut Tuttle clabbers my blood. Besides, I've already figured out the occupation I'll choose. Just call me Ollie Jolly, Rodeo Clown."